To Margaret and Diane ~ E B

For Roger Aylen ~ T M

LITTLE TIGER PRESS
An imprint of Magi Publications
1 The Coda Centre, 189 Munster Road, London SW6 6AW
www.littletigerpress.com

First published in Great Britain 2007
This edition published 2008

A CIP catalogue record for this book
is available from the British Library

Printed in Singapore

10 9 8 7 6 5 4 3 2 1

The Little Lost Robin

Elizabeth Baguley   Tina Macnaughton

LITTLE TIGER PRESS
London

On the edge of the deep wood lived an old hare. Once, he had leapt and pranced under the magical moon, but time had made him grey and stiff, and he no longer danced. Instead he spent his time looking out over the world, gently daydreaming.

Every day, Hare went to feed the small
brown birds, who chattered and chirruped.
Remembering his long-ago moondancing,
Hare tapped a merry paw to their busy tunes.
    One morning, in swooped a bird with
a berry-bright breast. "You're a bold little
robin," laughed Hare.

Even when autumn came, Hare still went
to share food with his friends. But then a
chill wind scattered the leaves, and the birds,
too cold to stay, flew far away.

Their song echoed with goodbye.

"I'll miss you, little birds," sighed Hare.

Then something made Hare prick up his ears.
A song! A song that lilted faintly, away in the
wood. It was a bird! Hare hurried towards the
fir tree where Robin shone scarlet, singing a
song warm as summer.

"Robin! You didn't fly away!"
exclaimed Hare.

And as Robin sang brightly,
Hare wound round in a slow dance.

"You've made this old hare feel
young again," he laughed.

So, every day, Hare would walk
into the blustery woods to bring
Robin seeds and sway to her song.

When winter arrived, freezing the wood and stiffening Hare's legs, Robin would come to the burrow to see him. Hare would wake as soon as the sun rose, and wait for her so that they could eat breakfast together.

"What would I do without you?" smiled Hare.

Then came a night that howled with storm-fury.
A wild wind exploded into the wood, blasting and
splintering trees. In whirled the snow, hiding the
land under its biting cold whiteness.

Deep in his burrow, Hare could not sleep for
worry about Robin. Had she been blown into the
storm, homeless and afraid?

At first light Hare rushed outside, hoping
that Robin would be waiting for him. But
there was no Robin, no Robin anywhere!
Where was she? Why hadn't she come?
Hare had to try to find her.

Out into the
snowy wood Hare
struggled. Finally he came
to Robin's tree and stopped.
It lay fallen, wrenched from the
ground by the storm.
"Robin!" he gasped. "Where are you?"
But, searching through the branches,
Hare found only her empty nest.

He slumped down, sure
that Robin was lost.

Just then, a tiny cheep made
him look up.

"Robin!" Hare shouted in
amazement. "I thought the
storm had taken you!"

As fast as she could, Robin flew to him.

"It's all right, little one," Hare said gently. "You can come back with me. I'll plant your tree outside my burrow, so you'll be quite at home."

The sun sank slowly as
Hare trudged home. Over
the humps and hollows of
snow he went, with Robin
nestled safely on his shoulder.

Back home, Hare helped Robin make
a new nest in the fir tree's branches.
Every day she warbled and whistled,
and when the night brought the light
of the magical moon, Hare joyfully
danced to her winter–bright tunes.

Lose yourself in these *brilliant reads* from Little Tiger Press

Gillian Lobel

Little Honey Bear and the Smiley Moon

Tim Warnes

STEVE SMALLMAN

THE LAMB WHO CAME FOR DINNER

JOËLLE DREIDEMY

Don't be Afraid, Little Ones

M Christina Butler   Caroline Pedler

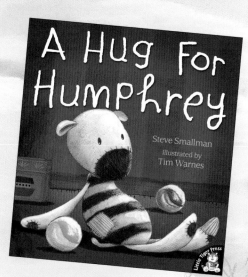

A Hug For Humphrey

Steve Smallman
illustrated by
Tim Warnes

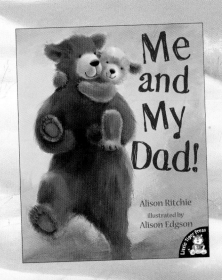

Me and My Dad!

Alison Ritchie
illustrated by
Alison Edgson

For information regarding any of the above titles
or for our catalogue, please contact us:
Little Tiger Press, 1 The Coda Centre,
189 Munster Road, London SW6 6AW
Tel: 020 7385 6333 Fax: 020 7385 7333
E-mail: info@littletiger.co.uk
www.littletigerpress.com